# Sticky Flies, Whirling Squirrels, and Plucky Ducks

FABLES RETOLD BY

# Eileen M. Berry

journey**forth**®

Greenville, South Carolina

**Library of Congress Cataloging-in-Publication Data**

Berry, Eileen M., date.
  Sticky flies, whirling squirrels, and plucky ducks / retold by Eileen M. Berry.
    p. cm.
    Summary: Thirty-one fables with Greek, Persian, Chinese, Russian, and Native American origins.
    ISBN 978-1-60682-009-4 (perfect bound pbk. : alk. paper)
  1. Fables. [1. Fables. 2. Folklore.]  I. Title.
  PZ8.2.B4694St 2009
  398.2—dc22

  [E]

2009014465

Illustrated and designed by Nathan Hutcheon

© 2009 by BJU Press

Greenville, SC 29614

JourneyForth Books is a division of BJU Press

ISBN 978–1–60682–009–4

15  14  13  12  11  10  9  8  7  6  5  4  3  2  1

# INTRODUCTION

Fables are short stories, often about animals, that make a point in an interesting way. A fable states its point in a brief closing sentence called the moral. The characters in a fable often make mistakes because of their wrong thinking and actions. We might even laugh at the funny things that happen to them. But when we take a look at the way they think and act, we can keep from making those same mistakes ourselves. A good fable always makes us a little wiser.

The fables in this collection come from many different parts of the world. The Greeks were the first to make fables popular. Many of these fables come from Aesop, a slave who lived in ancient Greece. Others come from the Persian, Chinese, Russian, and Native American peoples. Fables often reflect the beliefs of the people they come from. The fables in *Sticky Flies, Whirling Squirrels, and Plucky Ducks* were chosen because their morals reflect truths found in God's Word.

# CONTENTS

# THE FLIES AND
# THE HONEY POT

A pot of honey had been upset in a shop, and the flies swarmed in to eat it up. None of the flies would move from the spot while there was even one drop of honey left to eat. But after a while their feet became so sticky that they could not fly away. One by one, they began to smother in the luscious sweet liquid.

"We are miserable creatures," said one. "For the sake of an hour's pleasure we have thrown away our lives!"

*Greediness has its costs.*

# THE BOY SWIMMING

A boy was swimming in a river. Getting too far out, he was beginning to sink when he saw a traveler passing by. The boy called out for help with all his might. The man began to give the boy a lecture for his folly. But the boy cried out, "Please save me now, sir, and give me the lecture afterwards!"

*First things first.*

# THE WAR HORSE AND THE DONKEY

A war horse adorned with his fine trappings came thundering along the road. A poor donkey, trudging along the same road with a heavy load on his back, glanced up at him with envy.

"Get out of my road," said the proud horse, "or I shall trample you under my feet."

The donkey said nothing, but quickly moved to one side to let the horse pass.

Not long afterwards the regal war horse was called into battle, where he was badly wounded. He was no longer fit for military service, and he was sent to work on the same farm where the donkey worked. When the donkey saw this war horse dragging a heavy wagon, the donkey realized that he had been wrong to envy him.

Because of the war horse's proud spirit in his time of prosperity, he had lost the friends who might have comforted him in his time of need.

*Do not envy the proud.*

# THE VAIN JACKDAW

A conceited jackdaw found some peacock feathers, picked them up, and stuck them in among his own. Despising his old friends, he found a flock of beautiful peacocks and introduced himself to them with the greatest assurance.

Instantly the peacocks began whispering among themselves. "He's an intruder. Strip him of those borrowed feathers!" Falling upon him with their beaks, they plucked out the peacock feathers and sent him away.

The jackdaw, greatly humiliated and sorrowing deeply, returned to his jackdaw friends. He tried to join their flock again as if nothing had happened. But they remembered the proud airs he had put on and quickly dismissed him from their company.

"If you had been content with your lot," said one of them, "you would have escaped the punishment of your betters and the contempt of your equals."

*Beware of thinking too highly of yourself.*

# THE MILLER, HIS SON, AND THEIR DONKEY

A miller and his son were driving their donkey to a neighboring town fair to sell him. They had not gone far when they met a troop of girls returning from the town, talking and laughing. "Look," cried one of them, "did you ever see such fools, trudging along the road on foot when they could be riding?"

The old man, hearing this, quietly ordered his son to get on the donkey, and he walked along merrily beside him. They came up to a group of old men in earnest debate. "There," said one of them, pointing. "It proves what I was saying. No one has respect for old age these days. Do you see that idle young man riding while his old father has to walk? Get down, you rascal! Let the old man rest his weary limbs."

The father made his son dismount and got up himself. They had not gone much farther down the road when they met a company of women and children. "Why, you lazy old fellow!" cried several tongues at once. "How can you ride on the beast, while that poor little lad can hardly keep up with you on foot?"

"I stand corrected," said the good-natured miller. He pulled his son up onto the donkey behind him. They had now almost reached the town.

"Please, honest friend," said a townsman, "is that your own donkey you're riding?"

"Yes," said the old man.

"Oh, I would not have thought so by the way you load him down," said the townsman. "Why, you two fellows are better able to carry the poor beast than he is to carry you!"

"Anything to please you," said the old man. So he and his son got down and tied the donkey's legs together. They hung him from a pole which they carried between them on their shoulders. As they tried to carry him over a bridge that led into town, a crowd gathered to see the entertaining sight. The donkey, liking neither the noise nor his position, kicked apart the cords that bound him, tumbled off the pole, and fell into the river.

The old man, angry and ashamed, hurried home on foot with his son. "In trying to please everyone, I have pleased no one," he told his son. "And I've lost my donkey in the bargain."

*He who tries to please all, pleases none.*

# THE KING AND THE PEARL

A wealthy Arabian king was given a present—a pearl of great beauty and value, set in a ring. Shortly afterwards came a dry season in the land. The crops failed, and there was great suffering among his people. Moved with compassion, the king ordered that the pearl should be sold, and the money received for it should be given to the poor.

One of his friends reproached him for doing this. "Never again will such a beautiful jewel come into your hands," he told the king.

The king answered, "When a king wears an ornament while his people are poor and hungry, that ornament becomes ugly. Better for me is a stoneless ring than a suffering people."

*Happy is the man who sets the welfare of others above his own.*

# THE SQUIRREL AND THE THRUSH

A squirrel, the cherished pet of a rich man, was running in the whirling wheel of its cage. A thrush, perched outside on a tree branch, stared at the squirrel through the window of the rich man's home. The thrush was amazed. The squirrel ran so fast that his feet seemed invisible, and his bushy tail spread itself straight out behind him.

"Dear old friend of my native woods," said the thrush, "will you please tell me what on earth you are doing?"

"My dear fellow," replied the squirrel, "I have no time to stop and talk. I have to work hard all day. I am the courier of a great nobleman, and I can hardly stop to eat or drink or even catch my breath." And immediately the squirrel began again, running faster than ever in his wheel.

"Yes," said the thrush as he flew away, "I can see plainly enough that you are running. But for all that, you remain right there at the same window."

*One who thoughtlessly rushes about makes very little progress.*

# THE DOG AND THE SHADOW

A dog had stolen a piece of meat from a butcher's shop. As he was crossing a river on his way home, he saw his own shadow reflected in the stream below. *There's another dog with another piece of meat,* he thought. *I will get that piece also.*

He opened his jaws to snatch at the other dog's treasure. But when he did, he dropped the meat he was carrying and ended up with nothing at all.

*Those who dream of having more might lose their grasp on what they already have.*

# The Farmer
## and The Stork

A farmer set up a net in his field to catch the cranes that came to feed on his newly sown corn. When he went to examine the net and see how many cranes he had captured, he found a stork among them.

"Spare me," cried the stork, "and let me go. I am no crane. I have not eaten any of your corn. I am a poor innocent stork, as you see—the most dutiful of birds. I honor my father and mother. I—"

But the farmer cut him short. "All this may be true enough. But this I know, that I have caught you with the birds who were destroying my crops, and you must suffer with the company in which you are captured."

*You will be judged by the company you keep.*

# THE COUNTRY MOUSE AND THE TOWN MOUSE

Once upon a time a country mouse invited a friend from town to pay a visit to his country home. The town mouse accepted the invitation. The country mouse, though plain and rough and somewhat frugal by nature, generously opened his home and his heart to his old friend. He knew that his dainty guest had very elegant tastes. The country mouse brought every carefully stored-up crumb out of his pantry—peas, barley, cheese-gratings, and nuts. He hoped to make up in quantity for what he feared was missing in quality.

The town mouse picked at his food, eating a bit here and a bit there, while his host sat nibbling a blade of barley straw. Finally the town mouse said, "How is it, my good friend, that you can endure this dull, rough life? You are living like a toad in a hole. You can't really prefer these solitary rocks and woods to city streets teeming with carriages and men. You are wasting your time miserably here. We must make the most of life while it lasts. A mouse, you know, does not live forever. So come with me, and I'll show you the good life in town."

Overpowered with such fine words, the country mouse agreed. They set out together on their journey to town. It was late in the evening when they crept stealthily into the city, and it was midnight before they reached the great house where the town mouse lived. Inside were couches of crimson velvet, ivory carvings, and every other luxury. On the table were the remains of a splendid banquet.

It was now the town mouse's turn to play the host. He placed his country friend on a purple pillow. "You must try this and this and this!" he cried. Running back and forth from the table, he brought the country mouse dish after dish of dainty food. As though he were waiting on a king, he tasted every dish before he placed it in front of his friend.

The country mouse made himself quite at home, enjoying his good fortune. *What a poor, rough life I had before*, he thought. *I will never be able to go back to my peas and nuts after tasting this feast!*

Suddenly the door flew open, and a group of young people returning from a night out burst into the room. "This way!" the town mouse squeaked. The two frightened mice leaped from the table and scrambled to hide in the nearest corner. The young people moved on through the room into another. But no sooner did the mice venture to creep out again than some dogs began barking from a room nearby. The mice scurried back, more terrified than before.

Finally things seemed quiet. The country mouse stole out of his hiding place and quickly grabbed his hat and coat. "Goodbye, my friend," he said to the town mouse. "This life may suit you just fine. But give me my barley bread in peace and security rather than a dainty feast where fear and anxiety are waiting." And with that, he returned to his home in the country.

*Crumbs in comfort are better than a feast with fear.*

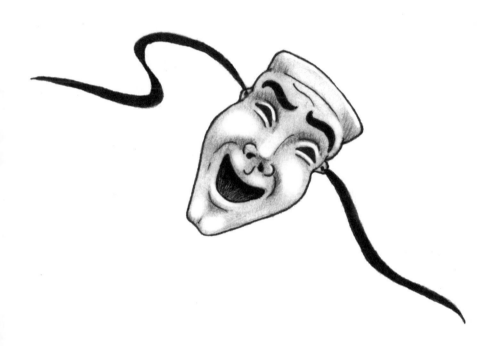

# THE FOX AND THE MASK

A fox stole into the house of an actor. Rummaging among his various props, the fox found a handsome mask. "A fine-looking head, indeed!" he cried. "What a pity that it lacks brains!"

*A fair outward appearance is a poor substitute for inward beauty.*

# THE LION AND
# THE SHEPHERD

A lion, roaming through a forest, stepped on a thorn. The pain in his paw was so great that he knew he would soon be unable to walk. Up ahead in a clearing, a shepherd was sitting on a rock. The lion limped up to him, lay down on the ground, and rolled over on his back with his paw in the air. "Now that is strange behavior for a lion," the shepherd said. He boldly examined the lion's paw and found the thorn. Placing the paw in his lap, he gently pulled the thorn out. Immediately the lion was relieved of his pain, and as suddenly as he had come, he disappeared into the forest again.

Some time later, the shepherd was falsely accused and put in prison. "Your crime is very great," the judge told him. "You are condemned to be thrown to the lions as your punishment."

The day came, and the condemned shepherd was led into the arena to be killed. But the lion, being released from his cage, recognized the shepherd as the man who had healed him. Instead of attacking him, he approached and softly placed his paw on his knee.

The news of the strange event reached the king. He listened to the tale and then gave orders to his servants. "See that the lion is set free again in the forest," he said, "and let the shepherd be pardoned and restored to his friends."

*A person known for his kindness will find favor even with his enemies.*

# THE LEAVES
### AND THE ROOTS

On a beautiful summer day the leaves of a tree whispered softly to the breezes. As the shadows fell across the valley, the leaves boasted of their beauty and abundance.

"Isn't it a fact that we are the pride of the whole valley? It is because of us that this tree is so wide-spreading and stately. What would it be without us? With our cool shade, we protect the shepherd and the traveler from the noonday heat. With our beauty we attract the shepherdesses to come and dance here. From among our leaves, both morning and evening, the nightingale sings. And you, gentle breezes, can hardly ever bear to leave us."

"You might spare just a word of thanks to us," interrupted a faint voice from underground.

"Who is that talking down there beneath the grass?" The leaves tossed on the tree with great disdain.

From far down below came the reply. "We are the ones who burrow here in the darkness to provide you with food. Is it possible that you do not know who we are? We are the roots of the tree on which you flourish. Go on rejoicing in your beauty! But remember there is this difference between us. Every autumn the old leaves die, and every spring new leaves are born. But if the roots perish even once, neither you nor the tree can live at all."

*Before you boast of your strengths, remember those who have made you strong.*

# The Wealthy Man and His Jewels

A wealthy man had a fine collection of jewels. He kept them hoarded away in a box, and he was very proud of them. He was constantly adding to the collection. One day he invited a friend to see the jewels. His friend feasted his eyes on the glittering gems for a long time.

"Well, I must go," the friend said at last. "Thank you very much for the jewels."

"What do you mean?" cried the man. "You must have misunderstood! I have not given the jewels to you. Why do you thank me?"

"Well," said his friend, "I have had as much pleasure from looking at the jewels as you can possibly have. The only difference between us that I can see is that I am free from all care, while you have the trouble of guarding them."

*The greater a man's treasures, the greater his cares.*

# The Mouse and the Frog

A mouse formed an unfortunate friendship with a frog, and they set off traveling together. The frog pretended to have great affection for the mouse. "I wouldn't want any harm to come to you, my dear friend," he said. "Tie your forefoot to my hind leg so I can be sure not to lose you along the way."

The mouse obeyed and hobbled along behind the frog for a while. Soon they came to a stream. "Take courage, my friend," said the frog. "We must swim across. Stay close behind!"

Being tied to the frog, there was not much else the mouse could do. The frog began to swim, and the mouse floundered along behind. He sputtered and fought to keep his nose above water. Just as they arrived at the middle of the stream, the frog took a sudden plunge to the bottom, dragging the poor mouse after him.

Desperately the mouse thrashed and splashed. His struggling made such a great commotion that a hawk noticed it. Swooping down, the hawk picked up the mouse in his beak and carried him off. Of course, the frog was forced to come along too, dangling below.

*Choose your friends with care.*

# THE WIND AND THE SUN

A dispute arose between the wind and the sun. "I am stronger than you," said the wind. "I can lift objects off the ground and set them down somewhere else. That is more than you can do."

"You *are* strong," said the sun. "But I think in a contest between the two of us, you would find that I am stronger."

"Let's settle the point then," the wind blustered. "See that traveler walking along the road? Whichever of us can make him take off his coat soonest is truly the stronger one."

"Fair enough," said the sun. "You begin."

The wind began and blew with all his might— a cold, fierce blast. But the stronger he blew, the closer the traveler wrapped his cloak around him, and the tighter he grasped it with his hands.

"Now it is my turn," said the sun.

The sun broke out from behind the clouds and beamed down on the traveler. Heating up to his warmest glow, the sun frightened away the damp air and the cold. The traveler felt the pleasant warmth and loosened his grasp on his coat.

As the sun shone brighter and brighter, he sat down, overcome with the heat, and threw off the coat completely.

"You have conquered fairly," said the wind. "Now I see that persuasion is better than force."

*A kind and gentle manner will open a man's heart sooner than all the threats in the world.*

# THE WOLF AND THE LION

A wolf roaming by a mountain at sunset saw his own shadow become greatly enlarged. He said to himself, "Why should I, being so immense and extending nearly an acre in length, be afraid of the lion? Shouldn't I be considered king of the beasts?"

While he was indulging in these proud thoughts, a lion attacked him. As the wolf lay dying, he exclaimed with regret, "Poor fool that I was! By thinking too well of myself I have brought about my own end."

*Pride goes before destruction.*

# THE MONKEY HOLDING COURT

The wolf once accused the fox of stealing from him. The fox was furious. "I have not stolen anything from you!" she said.

"We do not know who to believe," said the other animals. "Both the wolf and the fox are known for their dishonesty. Let's take the case to Judge Monkey. He will settle the dispute."

The two were brought before the judge. When each in turn had stated his side of the case, Judge Monkey looked sharply at both of them.

"It is evident, Mr. Wolf, that you have *not lost* what you ask back. But it is equally evident, Mrs. Fox, that you *did take* what you so furiously deny."

*It is difficult to learn the truth from those who rarely speak it.*

# THE WOLF AND THE CRANE

A wolf had a bone stuck in his throat. Coughing and sputtering, he ran through the forest, asking every animal he met to help him. "Please," he said, "won't you help me remove this bone from my throat? I'm offering a handsome reward to anyone who can pull it out!"

Most of the animals scampered away to their hiding places when they saw the wolf coming. But a crane, hearing his pleas and promises, liked the idea of a handsome reward. She flew down from a tree and landed beside the wolf. "May I try?" she asked.

The crane ventured her long neck down the wolf's throat and drew out the bone. "There!" she said. "Now, if you please, sir, the reward that you mentioned?"

The wolf grinned, showing his fierce-looking teeth. "Ungrateful creature! Do you ask for any other reward than this: you have put your head into a wolf's jaws, and you have come safely out again?"

*Those who give only in the hope of getting something in return will often be disappointed.*

# THE HORSE AND THE DONKEY

A man owned a horse and a donkey. Often when he traveled, he would place his entire load of goods on the donkey's back and spare the horse. One day the donkey, who had been ill for quite some time, begged the horse to relieve him of part of his load. "If you would take a fair portion, I would soon get well again," said the donkey. "But if you refuse to help me, this weight will kill me."

The horse shook his head. "You are just lazy," he said. "Now move along, and stop troubling me with your complaints."

The donkey jogged on in silence. Before long he was overtaken with the weight of his burden, and just as he had predicted, he dropped down dead.

The master loosened the load from the dead donkey and put it on the horse's back. Then on top of that burden, he made him carry the donkey's carcass.

"If only I had not been so ill-natured!" said the horse. "By refusing to bear my fair share of the load, I now have to carry the whole thing, with a dead weight into the bargain."

*Refuse to help, and you punish yourself as well as the one you refused.*

# THE FOX AND THE ICICLE

A hungry fox, searching for food one winter day, found a long, fine icicle. It was shaped very much like a bone. He began gnawing on it. But the more he gnawed, the more the bone seemed to be disappearing. Finally he gave up in frustration.

"A plague upon it!" he said. "It sounds like a bone in my ears, and it feels like a bone between my teeth, but never a scrap of it goes down into my stomach!"

*We must not judge by appearances.*

# THE WIND AND THE DUCK

On a bitterly cold winter day, the northwest wind saw a solitary duck searching for her food. She had found the few holes still remaining in the ice near the shore of a great bay and was diving through them.

"What folly," blustered the wind, "to try to resist me. I have driven every other living creature away."

The wind blew so hard and so cold that he froze over all the remaining holes. The poor little duck was forced to take shelter under the overhanging bank. Satisfied with his success, the wind retired, whistling, to his faraway home in the mountains.

When he arose the next morning, he found to his surprise that the duck had discovered some new holes. She was pushing the reeds out of her way and diving as cheerfully as ever.

"I must put a stop to this," howled the wind. "No duck is going to get the best of me!"

So for a whole week the wind blew, harder and harder every day. But each morning when he arose, he found the little duck steadily at work. She would break new holes with her beak, or else patiently wait for the ice to drift out of her way. Each day she kept finding her food as best she could. At last the wind said to himself, "Such plucky persistence deserves success. I may as well leave the duck in peace."

*Good comes to those who work hard and patiently endure.*

# The Rain Cloud

A large cloud passed rapidly over a hot, dry country but did not let a single drop fall to refresh it. Soon this same cloud poured a generous shower of rain into the sea. Then it began to boast of its generosity in the hearing of a neighboring mountain.

But the mountain replied, "What good have you done by such mistaken generosity? If you had poured your showers over the thirsty land, you would have saved a whole district from hunger. But as for the sea, my friend, it has plenty of water already, without your adding a few little raindrops to it."

*Give where the gift is needed most.*

# THE CRAB AND THE FOX

A crab on the seashore saw a beautiful green meadow in the distance. "How much nicer to be in that cool meadow than here on this hot, dry sand! I'm sure there would be tastier things to eat over there. I will go to that meadow and see what I can find."

He left the seashore and journeyed to the meadow. But shortly after he arrived, a hungry fox came along. "What a surprise," the fox said. "I've found a delicious crab for my supper without having to go near the sea."

The crab saw that there was no way to escape. When he realized that he was going to be eaten, he said, "I guess I've brought this upon myself. What business did I have on land, when by my nature and habits I am suited only for the sea?"

*Contentment with our lot is an element of happiness.*

# THE CROW AND THE PEACOCK

One day the peacock said to the crow, "This is Lord Tiger's wedding day. How shall we dress for the wedding?"

At that time the crow was white and the peacock yellow like a hen.

"I have an idea," the crow replied. "The king is having a house built. It is a wonderful house decorated in all the colors of the rainbow—green, red, yellow, and blue. The workmen have gone away to eat lunch. We will run and get their pots of paint."

The crow immediately put his idea into action.

"You paint me first," said the peacock.

The crow, wishing to show his ability, painted on the peacock's feathers moons of yellow and green and arabesques of blue and black.

The peacock was magnificent. He went to look at himself in the water of the river, spreading out his tail to dry his feathers. But when he saw how handsome he was, he continued to spread his tail, even after his feathers were dry.

"How beautiful I am!" he cried.

Just then the crow called to him, "Friend, it is your turn to show your cleverness."

But the peacock was proud. He had no intention of decorating the crow for Lord Tiger's wedding. So he said, "Didn't you hear the cry of that eagle? Danger! Let's run and hide ourselves!"

Pretending great haste, he ran against the pots of paint and knocked them into the river.

"I did not hear an eagle cry," said the crow.

"Then I must have been mistaken. Come, I will paint you."

"The paint is at the bottom of the river," the crow said.

The peacock nodded his head toward the last pot of paint left on the riverbank. "Here is one pot still left."

"Then hurry," said the crow. "Paint me before we are late to the wedding!"

The peacock quickly brushed a thick coat of paint over the crow's feathers. "There—you're lovely!"

The crow went to look at himself in the water of the river and found that he had been cruelly deceived. He wanted to complain; but his voice choked in his throat, and he could only scream harshly, "Caw! Caw!"

Ever since then crows have been black and have had a harsh voice. Peacocks are gorgeous with a thousand colors, but their voice is no better for that!

*Fine feathers do not necessarily make fine birds.*

# THE OLD WOMAN
## AND THE PHYSICIAN

An old woman had become blind, so she called in a physician. "If you will restore my eyesight," she said, "I will give you a handsome reward. But if you do not cure me, you will receive nothing."

"I accept your bargain," said the physician. From time to time, he tinkered with the old lady's eyes. But every time he visited her, he also carried off some of her furniture, paintings, and jewelry. After a time he began to treat her eyes in earnest and cured her. He asked for the promised reward.

But the old woman, recovering her sight, saw that her goods had been stolen from her house.

When the physician pleaded with her for his payment, she kept putting him off with excuses. At last he summoned her before the judges. When the judge called on her for her defense, she said, "What this man says is true enough. I promised to pay him a generous fee if my sight were restored, and nothing if my eyes continued bad. He says that I am now cured, but I say I can't possibly be. Before my blindness came on, I could see all sorts of furniture and goods in my house. But now when he says he has restored my sight, I cannot see a single one of them."

*He who deceives must be prepared for the consequences.*

# THE LION AND THE GOAT

On a summer's day when everything was suffering from extreme heat, a lion and a goat came at the same time to a puddle to quench their thirst. They began quarreling about which of them should drink of the water first. They could not resolve their quarrel, and it seemed that each was determined to resist the other . . . even to death.

Pausing in their quarrel to catch their breaths, they saw a flock of vultures hovering over them, waiting to pounce on the one who would die of thirst the soonest.

The lion and the goat looked at each other for a moment. Then at the same time, they both backed away from the puddle to let the other drink. "Let's be friends," said the lion.

"Yes," said the goat. "It's better to give up our quarrel than to furnish food for the vultures."

*Unresolved quarrels with our friends can make us prey for our enemies.*

# The Miser

A wealthy man wanted to make sure he kept all of his possessions for himself. He sold all that he had, converted it into a great lump of gold, and hid it in a hole in the ground. Every day he went to visit the hole to inspect his gold. This roused the curiosity of one of his workmen. Suspecting that there was a treasure, he went to the hole when his master's back was turned and stole the lump of gold.

When the miser returned and found the place empty, he wept and tore his hair. But a neighbor saw him and learned the cause of his great grief. "Do not fret over the gold any longer," he told the miser. "Take a stone and put it in the same place, and *imagine* that it is your lump of gold. Since you never meant to use the gold anyway, a stone will do just as well."

*The worth of money is not in possessing it, but in using it for good.*

# THE LION AND THE MOUSE

A lion was sleeping in his lair. A mouse, not looking where he was going, ran over the mighty beast's nose and awakened him. The lion clapped his paw down on the frightened little creature.

"Please, Mr. Lion," said the mouse in a muffled voice, "spare my life. Honestly, I did not mean to offend you. It would not be right for you to stain your honorable paws with so insignificant a prey as myself." His teeth chattered as he spoke this last sentence.

The lion smiled at his tiny prisoner's fright. Then he lifted his paw. "I'm feeling generous, my little friend," he said. "You may go."

Not long afterwards, as the lion was stalking through the woods, he fell into a hunter's trap. The more he tore at the ropes with his claws, the more he found himself entangled with no hope of escape. The lion set up a roar that echoed through the whole forest.

The mouse recognized the lion's voice and remembered his kindness that day in the lair. The mouse ran to the spot and set to work nibbling the knots in the lion's ropes. In a short time the ropes fell off, and the lion was free.

*When someone is kind to you, look for a way to return the kindness.*

# THE WILD BOAR AND THE FOX

A wild boar was sharpening his tusks against a tree. A fox passing by stopped to watch. "I see no reason why you should be doing this," the fox said. "There is neither hunter nor hound in sight, nor any other danger that I can see."

"True," replied the boar, "but when danger does arise, I shall have more important things to do than sharpening my weapons."

*It is too late to sharpen the sword when the time comes to draw it.*

# The Eagle
## and The Arrow

An archer took aim at an eagle and hit him in the heart. As the dying eagle turned his head, he saw that the arrow was winged with his own feathers. "How much sharper," said he, "are the wounds made by weapons which we ourselves have supplied!"

*We often give our enemies the means for our own destruction.*